Judge Rabbit
Helps the Fish

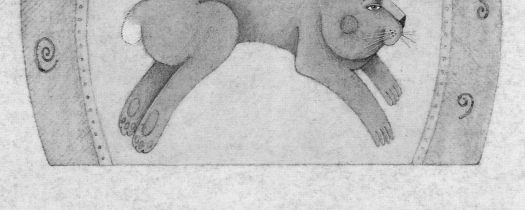

A tale from Cambodia retold by Cathy Spagnoli
Illustrations by Kat Thacker

Pel yu kun loong...

One day long ago in Cambodia, a hungry jackal hunted for food.
The monsoon rains had not come, and the rice fields were very dry.
So the jackal, ready to die, searched on

and on

and on.

Suddenly he saw a pond, dreaming of water but covered with mud.

And sticking out of that mud were tiny claws and flapping fish tails.

All the small creatures who lived there were trapped, with no place to hide.

"Ah," said the jackal, grinning. "THIS IS my LUCKY DAY! Here is my dinner just waiting for me!"

A clever shrimp heard the jackal
and thought quickly.

"Greetings, friend jackal!" he called. "You look too skinny today. You really need to eat us. But we're covered with mud now and not very tasty. Why not rinse us off first?"

"Yes, I should," said the jackal with a sigh, "but how? There is no water."

"Oh, that's easy," said the shrimp. "Near here is a big pond. It will still have water. Carry us there. We'll wash off, and you can enjoy a fine,

                fresh

                  meal."

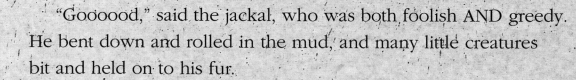

"Goooood," said the jackal, who was both foolish AND greedy. He bent down and rolled in the mud, and many little creatures bit and held on to his fur.

Then he walked slowly,
licking his lips.
　　When he got to the pond,
his passengers wriggled off.
　　"Now, go back for the others,"
said the shrimp. "We'll wait here."
　　And everyone lined up at the edge
of the pond.

With his stomach growling, the jackal soon brought the rest.
He let them slide off. Then he shook himself and lay down
near the water.

He opened his mouth wide, ready to eat
all those clean creatures.

WHEEE

But suddenly, with a *WHEEE* and a *WHOOSH*,

his dinner

dived

down

and disappeared!

WHOOSH

"Errrrrr!" snarled the jackal. "They're gone! They tricked me! But I'll get them. I'll ask the other animals to help, too."

And off he raced.

"Friends!" he barked. "I've been fooled by those water beasts.
Come help me catch them, and we'll have a fish feast!"
The forest dwellers heard, and
stomping, swaying,
flying, and playing,
they gathered together to plan.

"First," said a deer,
"we must drain the pond.
But how?"

"I can spray away so-o-o-o
much water with my big trunk,"
bragged the elephant.

"I'm s-s-s-strong and long,"
said the python, slithering.
"I can be a dam to keep
water back."

"We'll help, we'll help,
we'll help, too," chattered
the birds and the monkeys.
"We'll carry water,
we will, we will."

15

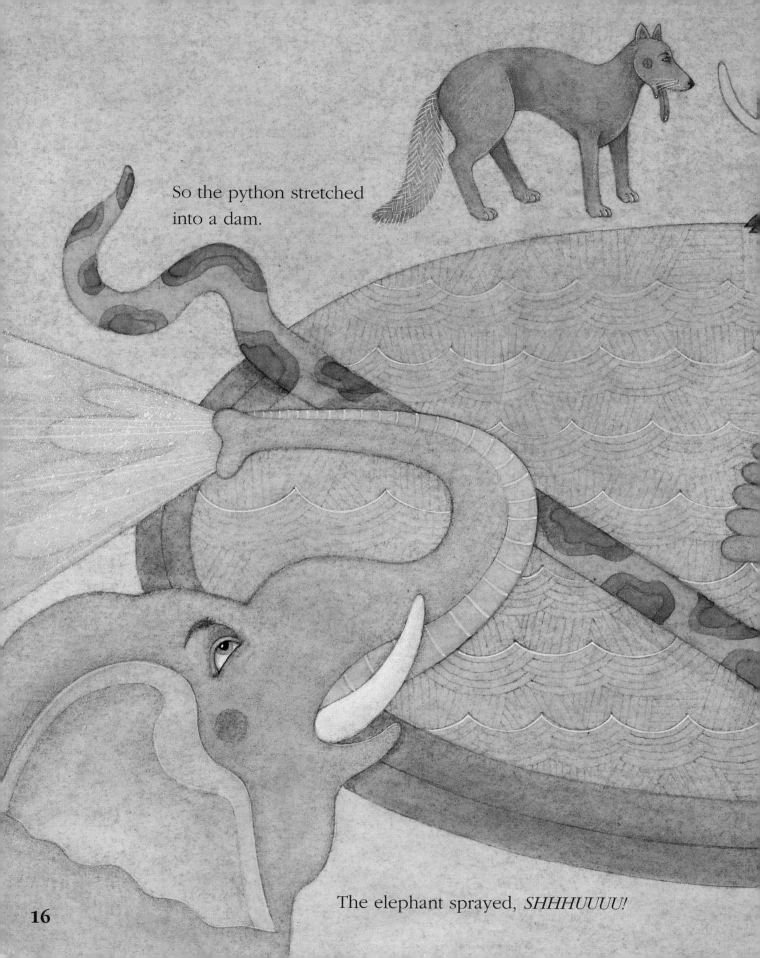

So the python stretched
into a dam.

The elephant sprayed, *SHHHUUUU!*

16

The deer and
monkeys scooped,

koop,

koop,

koop.

Birds filled beaks,
then flew off.

Little by little,
the water
left the pond.

17

Huddled in the bottom,
the water creatures watched
their new home grow smaller
and smaller
and smaller.

"Uh-h-h, I'm scared,"
cried a baby crab.
"What can we do?"

"Nothing," sniffed a snail.
"They're *too* big
and *too* strong."

"Wait! I have an idea!"
an old shrimp said.
"We can ask Judge Rabbit.
He knows so much and
always helps those in
trouble."

"I'll go find him,"
offered the kr'an fish.
"I can move on land
for a little while."
And the brave fish
slipped out of the water
into the grass.

"S-s-s-stop your shouting,"
said a water snake.
"There's-s-s-s a problem!
Judge Rabbit lives-s-s-s
far away."

"Yes, yes! Hooray!"
everyone yelled at once,
clapping their pincers
and claws.

19

Ka-blum, ka-blum, she bumped as she hurried along. Brother Sun above opened his eyes very wide. The fish soon felt so thirsty and so, so tired. But she remembered her friends and kept going until she heard—

Tchaa Tchaa

The Kr'an fish stopped near a rabbit who was sitting on a stump, munching a cucumber.

"What are you doing here, Sister Fish?" asked Judge Rabbit, blinking his wise eyes.

"Oh, Judge Rabbit," cried the fish, "PLEASE HELP! We're in GREAT TROUBLE. The big animals want to eat all of us who live in the pond."

Judge Rabbit scratched his ears, wiggled his nose, and said, "All right, I'll come."

The fish hopped back to share the good news,
and Judge Rabbit followed her to the pond.
There he watched the animals spray,

scoop,

fill,

and fly.

He saw that the pond was nearly dry. So he looked around
on the ground and found some large leaves. He picked up
the biggest one. It was covered with worm holes.
And those holes made designs that looked like letters.

Holding the leaf in both paws, Judge Rabbit
stepped on a mound and stretched his ears up proudly.
Then, rather loudly, he cleared his throat: "H-mmm, h-mmm!"
    And in a royal voice, he proclaimed:
"My friends, I have a message here from Indrea, the Great Ruler."
    Much surprised, the animals stopped their work and listened.

Judge Rabbit then pretended to read the leaf:

I, Indrea, will soon come to save those in the pond.
I will pull the elephant's trunk,
cut the monkey's hair,
tweak the bird's feathers,
and twist—

Kru kru kru,
the birds flew away.
They had heard
enough.

Kru kru kru

—and twist the tail of the deer.
No one waited to hear any more.
They all rushed off, very scared!
The deer dived through bamboo.
Monkeys moved up palm trees.
The jackal jumped away, too.

"WOOOOM, WOOOOM, WOOOOM,"
roared the elephant as he ran.
But in his hurry he stepped on the python,
and the dam broke.

"Wsh-wsh-wsh," sang the water, flowing back over the pond dwellers. Tiny tails and claws waved in delight.

"*Akun, akun,* thank you, older brother," their voices bubbled through the water.

Judge Rabbit's teeth sparkled in a smile as he watched his friends swim peacefully again. He bowed a good-bye and hopped back home.

And there he lived happily for a long, long time,
helping many others, both big and small.